This
belon

In martial arts, students are taught to be courteous; to respect each other, opponents, instructors and senior students. Bowing and shaking hands is used to show respect to one another in martial arts.

COURTESY

Being nice to others. Being polite, well mannered and treating others how you would like to be treated.

Written by
Andy McFarlane

Illustrated by
Jessica Leech

Kip

THE KICKBOXING BEAR CUB

The special meeting

Design cover and
layout by Mary Dewar
at MD Creations,
Dunfermline.

Kip is a brown
bear cub. He is
small and fluffy.

With big blue eyes
and big round ears.

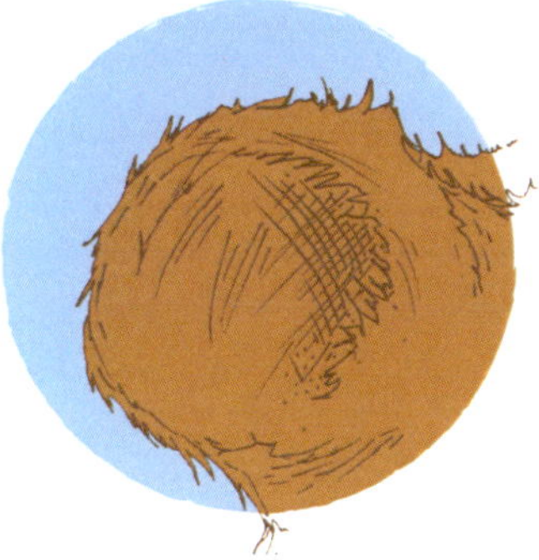

Kip lives in a den, made from fallen down trees, in a bear village in the heart of a pine forest.

High up in the Scottish Highlands.

One bright sunny morning, he was out playing hide and seek with his best friends Albi and Alba.

All of a sudden the three friends heard a noise coming from near where they were playing.

Stopping to listen, they could hear the sound of crying, but they couldn't see where it was coming from.

"Hello," they called out, and the crying stopped.

Kip listened carefully to where the noise had come from, and used his long nose to sniff out a scent.

He saw a bear cub that looked different from any bear cub he had ever seen, hiding in bushes near the river.

The bear cub had a big white coat, big teeth and big paws.

Albi and Alba were behind Kip and when they saw the white bear they looked at Kip, looked at the white bear and looked back at Kip.

Kip was a brave cub. He had been training as a kickboxer for a long time and one day hoped to be a blackbelt martial artist.

They were not sure what to make of the white bear, just as the white bear was not sure what to make of them.

Looking scared, the white bear tried to turn and hide further in the bushes.

“Hello, what is your name? I am Kip,” Kip said to the white bear, but the white bear just looked back at him.

“I think they’re scared,” Kip said to Albi and Alba, “I’m not sure if they can understand me.”

"I have an idea," Kip said. "I'll be back in a few minutes, wait here."

Kip walked into the forest, then reappeared with a pawful of berries.

"I'll offer the bear some berries, so they know we don't mean any harm," he said to Albi and Alba.

"How do you know they don't mean to harm us?" asked Alba.

"That is a good question Alba, but one of the values I learned through martial arts is courtesy," said Kip.

"Courtesy means you should treat others with respect, be kind and polite."

"We should treat this bear how we would want to be treated."

Kip ate some of the berries, then looked at the white bear. He put out his paw, smiled and offered the bear some berries.

The white bear came forward, looked at Kip, sniffed the berries and...

...then took some out of his paw and started eating them.

The bear looked back at Kip, still a bit frightened, but gave a wee smile.

Kip smiled at the white bear and asked again "What is your name?"

Kip brought his paw up and pointed to himself and said nice and slowly, "Kip."

The white bear brought their paw up, copying Kip and said "Ayla."

Kip's plan had worked. He knew that just because the bear looked different to him and his friends they would still feel the same way they would. He had acted with courtesy.

"Now" said Kip, thinking out loud
"Are you lost?"

"Are you here by yourself?"

"What will we all do now?"

Milton Keynes UK
Ingram Content Group UK Ltd.
UKRC030015270824
1390UKWH00004B/33

* 9 7 8 1 7 3 8 5 4 0 9 0 7 *